I0607985

The Lodestone Files

The Things in the Shadows

Among Us: Contact, Assimilation, Control, Extermination Series
Book One

ROBERT J. S. T. McCARTNEY

A.B.Normal Publishing and Media Group™

Publishing and Media Group

Anything but normal.

A.B.Normal Publishing and Media Group
PO Box 31311
Knoxville, TN 37930
www.abnormalpublishing.com

Publisher's note: This is a work of fiction. Names, characters, places, and incidents are a product of the author's imagination. Locales and public names are sometimes used for atmospheric purposes. Any resemblance to actual people, living or dead, or to businesses, companies, events, institutions, or locales is completely coincidental.

Book Layout © 2014 BookDesignTemplates.com

The Lodestone Files: The Things in the Shadows / **Robert J. S. T. McCartney** — Second Print, 2020

To my wife, Karyn, and my kids, Zelda, and Aeris.

Do what you want to do with your life. Go ahead, dream big, make plans, but get off your hands and make them happen.
—**Robert J. S. T. McCartney**

"Be anything but normal."
—**Robert J. S. T. McCartney**

CONTENTS

Be sure to look for these great titles and more.

Lilah's Guide to Hoyle by Robert J. S. T. McCartney and
Albert J. Debusschere III, available now.

Chapter One

THE SUN HAD already begun its descent upon the horizon. The stars ignited across the fading daylight and exploded into the template of the nightly majesty, which was no stranger. The moon high, full, and brilliant, even amidst the presently elegant summer evening. The skyline articulated with precise brushstrokes of pink, peach, and azure. The white caps of the clouds radiated a magnificence about them. If anything, it reminded him of his mother's valued peaches and cream milkshake, with the sun as the almighty cherry. While deep on the horizon's depths, there laid a siege of dark, foreboding, and ever-persistent storm clouds—tainted with something evil that weaved its magic in the neighboring county.

"Tonight's forecast calls for a high chance of rain. A severe thunderstorm watch is in effect for the following counties—" The newscaster's voice cut short as the signal gave way to the classical static snow.

Idris sighed as he readjusted his blue jean jacket and fixed his black t-shirt. His hands dug around in the pockets of his dark blue jeans, running the loose change through his fingertips while continuing to look at the morbid onslaught that seemed to creep closer with every passing moment. He was in awe at the traditional "night and day" that was transpiring before him. He roamed a bit further, standing under the covered fuel pump of the gas station, and took note of the swirling maelstrom of clouds that slowly wandered by on high. It had been some years since he last saw something of this magnitude, and he then remembered—death.

He glanced over at the old crimson fuel pump that stood proudly, garnished by a circle of different types of rocks, and various flowers in the small little acreage. At the base was a white cross with a white-flowered wreath that hung on it. Along the side of the fuel pump in beautiful white calligraphy read:

In Loving Memory Lawrence Calloway James Sinclair III
Beloved Son, Husband, Father, and Grandfather
May 21, 1912 – March 18, 2004

His eyes turned to the ground before him.

Grandpa...

Memories flashed before his eyes of an old man. White hair combed back, thin black wire-rimmed glasses that sat low on his small nose. He had a long slender face with sparse wrinkles—the wrinkles that were always present with his vibrant and warm smile. This memory, or rather recurrent recollection, he dressed in his usual brown silk vest over his silk grey-blue dress shirt, and black slacks and charcoal suede shoes. To Idris, he was more than the marveled superhero of their small haven. He vaguely recalled how their great-great-grandfather helped found soda fountains. Then his memory recalled the last root beer float they shared together days before...

Tears began to well up, when... *Ding! Ding!*

He snapped out of his moment of remembrance upon hearing the gas station bell chime. Another customer had come, and he knew it was unprofessional being emotional around patrons. The black 94' Ford Explorer came to a halt at one of the fuel pumps. Idris walked over, peered into the vehicle, as the drivers' window slowly lowered, revealing a middle-aged man, and his weary family.

"What will it be, sir?" Idris kindly inquired.

The man smiled in reply, "Fill it up, please."

Idris turned and reached for the gas nozzle. "Do you want any particular grade, sir?"

"Regular, please," the man replied before turning to his wife.

The man's family had gotten out, stretched their legs, and walked off to the station's diner. Idris unscrewed the fuel tank cap and put the nozzle in it. He went about doing the standard customary service: wiping the headlights, taillights, and all windows clean. He walked over and grabbed the air compressor hose, and set off to check the air pressure in each tire—topping off all four.

Idris came around to the driver's side once more. "Sir, if you'd like to join your family inside, I can move your vehicle for you."

"Oh-oh, why thank you, young man." The man smiled as he slowly got out of the vehicle, apparently stiffened from the long hours of road travel.

Robert J. S. T. McCartney

Idris smiled in reply. "No problem, sir. I can bring your bill inside. So, if you're purchasing a meal, you can take care of all of it at once."

The man chuckled. "Well, I wish we had more of this back home."

Idris gave a smile at the man. The customer turned to head inside the diner. He noted that it seemed the man had accepted his balding situation. He had shaved his head completely, except the light blonde mustache that was growing. The loud rustling of his black leather jacket as he swayed each step. Idris noticed he walked with a limp on his right leg, the imperfection of his light-brown slacks and uneven length suggested a possible amputee. Idris noted the Persian Gulf Veteran sticker on the rear window. He was familiar with all the 'benefits' veterans received, recalling that his uncle had served in a few wars himself.

Idris sighed, shaking his head.

After a moment's passing, Idris put the fuel cap back on and returned the nozzle to its holster. He read the amount on the gas pump and pushed a button on the gas pump.

A deep voice spoke from the small speaker. "Yes?"

Idris leaned towards the speaker. "Can you please pair the fuel receipt with a customer's dinner—a party of five."

There was a slight pause, and then the voice crackled in response. "Alright, kiddo, thanks."

Idris rolled his eyes, grumbling aloud. He hated being called kiddo. "What was that?" The voice sternly inquired.

"I said, 'no problem, dad.'"

I said I am not a kid anymore, you, half-wit, that's what.

"Oh, OK," he heard his dad chuckle. "Sorry, it's getting busy in here. You mind giving me a hand?"

Page |4

"Sure, just give me a few minutes." Idris then sighed to himself.

He opened the driver's door and hopped in the Explorer. He glanced briefly at the rear-view mirror. He resembled his grandfather more than his father. Dark green eyes tired from the long day and even longer coming night. He was tall, like most of the men in his family. Combed back short black hair which spoke of his professional mannerism, contrary to his usual wild look. As he turned the key, the engine turned over, and the beast growled with its unfamiliar driver. He changed the gear and set off to park in the front of the restaurant.

As he exited out of the parked vehicle, he heard a child's voice call out, "Idris!"

He looked up as he escaped the belly of the beast, keys in hand, at his kid brother. "Hey, Cal, how's it going, little man?"

Cal beamed in his brother's presence—proud and prideful. He was seven years younger than Idris, and already was beginning to shoot up like a weed. Cal resembled their father with his sandy brown hair and bright green eyes. His person dirty (apparently, he was helping Dad a lot today), food stains covered his white t-shirt and blue jeans, and sneakers. Cal held a brown paper bag in his right hand, smiling.

"Whatcha got there?" Idris smiled as he spun the keys in loops on his right index finger (visionary gunslinger with his kid brother as his faithful sidekick).

"I got you something since tomorrow's your birthday. I saved up some money and—"

"Cal, that's your money. You didn't have to get me anything." Idris sighed. "You know that, right? I rather you had spent it on yourself than me."

Cal puckered his lower lip. "Yeah, I know. It's my money, and I can decide what I want to do with it. I did earn it on my own after all."

Idris caught the small grin in the corner of Cal's face. Shaking his head—he was clearly wising up and catching on to his brother's wisecracks.

Idris sighed. "Alright, you got me." he walked over to his brother. "So, what did ya get me?"

Cal frowned, his tone sarcastic, "Really? That would kinda ruin the surprise of it all, you know."

Idris laughed. "Ah c'mon, Cal, I'm just messing with you." he ruffled his brother's hair. Cal giggled as he wrestled his brother's arm away. "Come on; I'll make you a root beer float. What do you say? Then I will open the gift you got for me."

Cal gave a big smile and a nod. The two brothers set off for the diner.

Upon entry into the restaurant, there laid a large rug that proclaimed 'Welcome!' It wasn't a typical welcoming mat. Oh no, this was a throwback, just like the way their father loved it. In the massive white circle was a gigantic chocolate milkshake, topped with whipped cream and a cherry on top. Above it, denoted the red letters that made up the welcome, as well as the bottom's 'to Calloway's and Family.' The outline of the circle resembled a bright-red neon sign, just all it needed now was to light up.

Stretched from beyond the doorways, was a black-and-white checkered tile that sprawled everywhere. Directly in front was a small bar with chrome and red bar stools, where a few patrons sipped on handcrafted malts and shakes. Behind it was four shelves of assorted drinking cups, shake and malt necessities, and their famous soda fountain. In the left corner was a classical jukebox that contained both vinyl records and digital recordings of songs, a project their father was proud to accomplish. It glowed in an array of chrome, red, blue, and green lights. The arch glowed a steady light-yellow in contrast to its light-brown base hue.

Above them, spun fans, lightly circulating the delicious smell that continued to permeate everywhere. Along each side were booths adjoined to the walls (white tabletops and black vinyl seating). A few tables spaced evenly across the floor, offering their black and white contrast of chairs and tables, respectively. All-around on the white walls hung memorabilia over the years from customers, Idris' family, and of course, his father. Neon signs were aplenty, traditional neon clocks, Coca-Cola, and a Calloway's and Family customized sign. The colors of the rainbow tamed and populated this little piece of heaven.

Inside, the diner was hopping, like it usually was. The smell of fresh cooked to order food slammed across your face like a sack of potatoes. Idris sniffed the air, immediately salivating. He could tell his dad was making his famous Six Shooter Slider Combo. The other servers and cooks were all busy, after all, it was Friday, and their dad's exceptional gut busters were always a hit. Idris stood there with Cal, and both just looked at their very own wonder of the world, as it all played out before them. It was like their own Willy Wonka factory, except with no Oompa Loompas and the place itself, definitely wasn't edible. Still, they admired their wonderful world and loved eating it. Their eyes wandered from side to side, taking in the spectacle of happy customers and memories in the making, and of course, the cash.

Their mother carried trays of food over to the middle-aged man's table. His two kids were sipping on cola while picking at the fresh French fries that steamed with wholesome goodness, big smiles on their faces. The man nodded and a smile to the two brothers.

Their mother came around and stopped in front of the boys. She wore a classic waitress outfit, but then again, their dad did have a thing for 50's diners. A white skirt fanned out from her waist and slung down to her knees, high enough from her black pumps that waltzed across the well-traveled tiled floor. A dark cloth belt sat above her waist, tucking in the light-blue short-sleeved shirt. There was no doubt; their mother did not belong in a restaurant, let alone the kitchen. Often Idris wondered if she was their mother with her classic supermodel glam. She had bright blue eyes that radiated with happiness, as well as a broad beaming smile. Her hair was up in a tight ponytail that bounced and shifted side to side. To them, she was their mom, but to customers, she was Mary.

"Hey Mom," Idris smiled at his mother, "guess we're busy now, huh?"

"Hi, honey," she smiled in reply. "Oh, it's not too bad. Your father could probably use a hand in the kitchen. Blaine had to leave early. Apparently, Stella just went into labor." Mary sighed. "But that's why we have you, boys! Free labor!"

The trio giggled amongst themselves.

"Yeah, I think we can help dad out." Idris nodded. "Afterward, I want to make Cal a root beer float. Y'know how Grandpa showed me."

Mary smiled. "I think that would be lovely, dear." She glanced at the busy dining room. "Well, I am going to get back. Money won't make itself! You boys be good now. You hear?"

To which both brothers replied, "Yes, ma'am."

Soon enough, their mother was off on her waitress's missions, leaving Cal and Idris alone at the entrance. Idris looked down at his little brother. "Ready to help dad some more?"

Cal nodded. "Maybe we can make something up for next week's special."

Idris smiled and chuckled. "Who knows, maybe we'll make something as good as what dad can make."

Soon enough, they set off themselves. Along the way, Idris put the man's keys with his assigned table on a pegged rack by the cash register, then continued for the kitchen. Inside, orders were being shouted out left and right, and pans clanged, banged. Deep fryers bubbled as fresh potatoes sank to their oil baths, a final destination: golden-brown and to a plate near you. Other pots and pans sizzled, while the grill was the prime spot, with their father at the reins.

"Hey, now there are my two favorite helpers!" Their father smiled, glancing at them briefly as he flipped a series of six square beef patties, and dressed them with sautéed onions.

Idris and Cal became enticed by the sweet aroma of pure perfection that sizzled before them. Their father then laid out buttered buns for each patty and began dressing them with a slice of American cheese.

He wore a white hat, like the diner hats of old, hiding, or at least obstructing his sandy brown hair. One half was 'James' in a bold black print, while the other half read 'Calloway's and Family.' He was tall, fit, and undoubtedly agile for the kitchen war front. The man could dance all over the kitchen and nearly run it solo. He was as Idris proclaimed, a beast. He was well-kept—clean, shaven.

Contrary to his white uniform, which was a bit dirty, but that was to be expected. Grease stains, ketchup, and more. It was collateral damage, but delicious. He ran his hands on his black slacks and wandered over to the sink. The sink billowed with steam as the water ran from the faucet.

James grabbed a towel and dried his hands. "So, you boys here to help?"

The brothers nodded in unison.

James smiled, "Great! Let me finish this order, and I'll set you two up." Their dad walked past them towards the grill, throwing the towel over his shoulder. "I'd like you both to make me something for next week's specials." He glanced at the boys giving them another vibrant smile.

Cal tugged on Idris' sleeve, smiling with glee. Idris smiled at Cal, taking off his jacket and setting off for getting dressed before grabbing the essentials for grilling.

Everything was going great. Life was good. The food was astounding, and it seemed like nothing could go wrong, not here, not for Idris and his family.

Until…

Chapter Two

IDRIS STROLLED AROUND the gas station in which he maintained. The station, which was a small little building that adjoined to the diner, contained the essentials—alcohol (both beer and liquor), soda, snacks, and assorted candies. It was well-kept, despite the other nearby stations that were a bit…run down. It was all about lower gas prices. Political agendas, something Idris, didn't care. Another reason he felt he shouldn't bother enlisting. Granted, he was thankful of his forefathers, and all those in his family that fought for the greater good, but nowadays, he would instead run the diner, then run off to war for someone else's ideals.

Here, it was quaint. It didn't have that motor oil smell or gas. White linoleum sprawled itself over the entire floor. A few rows—about five—of snacks and candy, while there were six coolers for beer, dairy, and soda. Those ran along the back corner, near the breezeway that led to the diner. In front of the front windows were small displays of soda, cases of beer, and chips. Prices marked down for easy customer purchase and near the exit for appropriate consumption (provided if it was alcohol, it stated on the small sign that was posted by the door and beer cases that "alcohol was not to be consumed on the premises"). Above the register—and even behind it—was the little tobacco and lotto nook (for the compulsive and hopeful gambler, and the everyday-down-on-their-luck worker) different cigars, cigarettes, snuff, chew, and various scratch-offs and the old lotto machine.

Mostly, this ideal hole in the wall (which ironically, it was from the diner's perspective), was a small slice of heaven-on-the-go. The back wall was a nice little meal slip containing— nachos, hot dogs, pizza, and other fresh made items. Nearby was a modern self-serve soda fountain, complete with plastic cups for consumer consumption, priced at remarkable prices that egged on to buy immediately. In stock, there were oversized mugs that offered more bang for your buck, promoting to buy one and get your favorite filled beverage free, or free with the purchase of select named hot n' fresh food-to-go.

Albeit, even though the station's food was freshly prepared, Idris and Cal always preferred going into their dad's diner and making something to eat. Who knows, it could lead to the menu or even the weekly special.

Idris smiled. He and his brother had crafted next week's special—Pepper jack cheese-stuffed burgers, with a pan-fried egg laid on the beefy bed. Garnished with the fixings: lettuce, pickles, tomato, onions, mayo, mustard, and ketchup (per customer's request, of course). The new gut buster went up to a triple stacked mountain, and could even be garnished with bacon. It was their first crown achievement that they had accomplished this month, and still, they had a plethora of ideas to grill out.

He reached into his coat pocket and pulled out a silver polished pocket watch, attached to it was a long small silver chain attached to the inside of his blue jean jacket. He smiled, reading the inscription his little brother had dedicated to him.

Here's to my big brother and fellow grill master, Idris. ~ Cal V

He tucked the watch back into his coat pocket and turned his gaze out. He peered through the window at the tan van that had remained in the parking lot. It had been a few days and still. He saw no one go near it.

He turned around and walked over to his father, who was busy counting money in the register. "Hey, Dad? Do you know whose van that is?"

"Twenty-three, twenty-four, hang on a moment, Idris, twenty-five, twenty-six..." his dad counted, putting large amounts of money in a small faded blue bag, along with a rubber band bound wad of white slips. "Alright," he zipped up the bag and looked down at his son. "now, what was your question?"

Idris sighed at his father. It wasn't uncommon for his dad to forget things when it came to 'family matters,' but when it came to tending the diner, let alone anything business-related, he was spot on. Especially when it came to the kitchen, James was like some unbound storm that thrashed wildly everywhere. You could rattle off a whole list of orders, and he could memorize everything to a T.

Idris walked over to his father, behind the gas station counter. "That van, do you know who's it is?"

James looked up, out through the station's window. "Hmm, not really. Did you ask your mom?"

Idris ran his palm over his face. "She said to ask you."

James chuckled lightly, "Ah, that woman," he sighed. "Well, I can take the plate down, and have the police run the plates, and say it was abandoned here. They can deal with it."

Idris nodded and turned around to look at the van.

It sure seems like there's an awful lot of stuff in there.

He was right, and his curiosity would get the best of him.

Chapter Three

NIGHT HAD COME at last, and the heavy rain was the least of his worries.

If dad sees me, my ass is grass.

He scanned the parking lot and saw no one in view. Everyone who parked was either help or being served in the diner. He walked over to the old light-brown van. He readied the slim jim. He fiddled with it a bit, remembering how his grandfather had taught him.

"The boy's gotta learn sometime, James. I can't tell you how many times I've saved money doing this myself. Hell, I could have done a roadside service!"

He grinned at the memory. At that time, he was thirteen. Of course, he did what any good-natured youth did, broke into a friend's car, and reclaimed his Lord of the Rings: Extended Edition DVD box cases. Idris, of course, used his powers for the greater good. That is if breaking into a car counted as a 'power.' However, not everyone was so understanding of his particular skills. For all he knew, this could have been a time bomb waiting to happen.

He fiddled some more and pulled up. A click and the door unlocked. "Still got it after all." He grinned.

He hopped inside, his eyes taking in all the strange things that littered the vehicle.

"When were you going to tell me?" He heard a familiar voice in the backseat.

Idris turned around in the drivers' seat. "Cal?! What are you doing here?"

Cal sat there, smiling at his ninja-like skills. "I got in here about five minutes ago."

Idris shook his head, "If dad catches us…"

Cal shook his head. "Dad's busy, and I think he might thank us for all that's in here. Look at all this stuff!" Cal pointed at the various boxes that polluted the back with the different guns, knives, rations, and more in the cargo hold.

"By the power of Grayskull." Idris' jaw dropped at the sight.

Cal rolled his eyes, noting he only said such a thing because of one of his favorite movies, and Idris insisted it was the best action-comedy flick ever made.

Idris scanned over the dashboard of the old van; assorted yellow sticky notes polluted the cheap plastic wood paneling. These notes all displayed specific dates and times, and of a test subject known only as the Thing. He glanced down at the center console. Reaching down, he retrieved a CD case titled The Crystal Rock-Ship. On the cover, was Queen, David Bowie, The Doors, and other bands.

Idris smiled to himself for finding such a rare gem. He had heard of this album from his father, only two hundred and fifty were produced for a private benefit concert and banquet. Very few knew the exact contents and further tarnished such exemplary music establishments—false or cheaply burned disks and other shoddy compilations. Plus, his father's copy was stolen when he was in Chicago some years back.

He pocketed the CD and continued to look around. In the back was a small surplus of assorted guns and other weaponry: boxes of ammunition, more files, and notes. He saw a tiny red light in the top left corner of the rear door.

"Hey, Cal, what does that say?"

A crudely written note below it stated that when aglow: 25 minutes until the other feds arrive.

Cal turned around and carefully read the note. "Something about 25 minutes until some other feds arrive."

What the hell does that mean?

As Idris pondered on the significance the light played, he saw it ignite into its cherry-red glow. The signal had already been made.

The two hopped out of the van and got their story together. James had started walking outside when he saw the two brothers.

"What the hell were you two doing?"

"Dad! You're not going to believe what kind of stuff is in here!" Cal piped, surprised by his father's sudden appearance.

"What are you doing out here, dad? Shouldn't you be in the diner with mom?" Idris calmly inquired.

James shook his head, sighing. "Just like your old man." He cleared his throat, "I asked you both a question."

Robert J. S. T. McCartney

Idris took a breath and calmly gave his answer. "I saw a red light in the back glowing, and there was a beeping sound. I thought it could be hazardous to the diner and the station. So, I checked it out, since it's abandoned, and no one has claimed it."

James looked at both boys, and then the van. Giving a nod, he folded his arms. "So? What's inside it, Sherlock?"

"A lot of shi—er, stuff, Watson." Idris casually replied.

Cal giggled, while their father shook his head.

"I almost regret ever allowing your Grandpa to show you how to use that thing." He sighed.

"Alright, well, let's take a look. I have yet to call the police, so maybe I can give more information about it."

James poked his head inside the van and searched the interior. "Holy hell, it's like a one-man army's supply depot."

Cal and Idris glanced at each other.

Their father pulled himself out of the van. "Did you boys take anything?"

Both replied in unison, "No, sir."

James eyed the two, studying them, and decided to believe them. "Alright, well, I'll look a bit more in here and then telephone the cops."

Idris had a nagging feeling eating at him. "Dad? There's a light in the back with a note that says in 25 minutes the other feds will arrive. Do you know what that means?"

James hesitated and seemed reluctant to answer. He muttered to himself something incoherent to the boys.

Idris took note of this. "What's the matter, dad?"

James shook his head. "Nothing, Idris. I found the owner's name here, so I'm going to phone the police and have them deal with it." He began to walk towards the station entrance and then turned around. "You two should get inside…I don't want anything to happen to you two.

Cal and Idris both shivered upon hearing this, and curiosity began to nip at them more and more.

They had snuck in the back door for shipping and receiving and were not far from their father's office. Both looked to one another in silence, trying to hear the conversation taking place.

"Hi, is this Cheryl Plain? I have a van here that I believe is yours. The police said you—oh…uh-huh…OK, thanks. Yeah, we'll be here." James hung up the phone and sighed heavily.

He picked the phone back up and then spoke urgently to whoever was at the end of the line. "Hey, yeah, it's me. Are you able to get us? Uh-huh, alright. If we don't, then the two will. Knowing him, he'll figure it out and know where you are. Thanks. Yeah, we're going to need it."

There was a silence, then a loud crashing sound against the wall. Idris and Cal immediately entered in response. They saw the phone smashed on the floor, and their father's desk cleared of everything.

"Dad, are you OK?" Idris inquired hesitantly.

James sighed heavily. "Yes, son."

"Well, what's the matter?"

"I need you to get your mother, and you two need to pack lightly. We need to leave. Lock the doors, and tell the last few customers to leave—that the meal is free. If they ask why, say there's an emergency in the town, and it requires an evacuation."

Idris and Cal both looked to one another, scared.

"Dad, what—"

James slammed his fist down on his desk. "Do what I say! Go now!"

It was a rare opportunity that their father would exercise anger, and this was not shaping up too well.

They did as their father asked them to do. No one questioned them, not even their mother. The customers had all taken their meals to go and hurried out to their vehicles promptly. The family headed to their little rooms to pack lightly. Then…it started. The power and the lights went out.

James looked to the ceiling with Mary. "Son of a bitch…"

Mary looked at James. "I'll get the boys."

James nodded. "OK, I'll get the gun and whatever else. We have to move quickly, though."

Together, they snuck out the back door, hoping to elude the fast-approaching silhouettes in the front. They panted as they pushed themselves hastily ran up the hill only to come to a dead stop. At first, they couldn't tell what laid before them. Maybe it was the thick fog that had suddenly crept across the town, or perhaps it was the uneasy feeling that tonight was the night that this family would be whole.

Their hairs on the necks stood up in the frigid evening, the rain had lightened up significantly. It seemed like a haunting was about to take place, as a hungry, thick, dreadful fog had set its eyes on this small family. No one made a sound. No one dared move. The confusion of the night's events still grasped at them all.

"What the hell are they?" their father whispered, his arms blocking his family.

Lazily, the dark silhouettes all drifted towards them. Fog shrouded, misshapen, and malformed marionettes—dancing to the ballet of sinister destruction and death. Waltzing their way towards their victims, and for what reasons? Series of crimson vines shimmered brilliantly under the twilight's veil to each limb, to each…thing. They all grinned, a most sinister grin, as they came closer every passing moment. Their eyes— it could be said they were lifeless—dull and black, as black as night itself; save for the moon's silver reflection in the whites of their eyes. However, every so often, there was a glimmer of something orange…fierce and sinister—a scanner assessing weaknesses and pinpointing precise measures of dealing death.

"What do you want from us?!" James shouted.

Still, they marched.

"Please, leave us alone! We never did anything to you!" Their mother pleaded.

Still, *they* marched.

Cal tugged on his big brother's arm. "Idris, what's going to happen to us?"

Idris looked down at Cal, restraining the fear—for himself, his parents, and his brother. "We're going to get out of here; that's what. Don't worry, Cal."

Cal smiled half-heartedly at his brother's assurance, but he was no fool.

Their father frantically searched about them for exploiting an opening. "Boys, I want you to take your mother and run. Now!"

"Dad, no, we can't just leave you!" Idris and Cal pleaded with their father.

"James, I am not going to leave you to—this—whatever the hell these things are!"

"Honey, just trust me. Take the boys and go. I will be okay. I promise."

James reached from behind his waist and pulled out a .45 revolver, his father's gun. He aimed for the things' head and fired a shot, dropping it to the ground.

"I said run, now!"

The boys and their mother turned around and hurried down the hill. James fired a few more shots and was sent tumbling down the hill.

"Dad, are you alright?!" Idris rushed to his father's side.

Together, the boys and their mother helped James to his feet.

"They ate—the ones—I killed," James panted, watching the top of the hill.

The boys looked at one another. At the peak of the hill, there were fewer things; however, a few were more sizable. More and more red vines seemed to protrude and lash about wildly around it. The eyes in these larger ones appeared to glow more like a raging fire, especially at their father.

James took a step back and nearly collapsed.

Mary searched her husband over. "What's wrong, James?"

"Ah, my leg, that red shit nearly tore it off. I can't feel it anymore." James' eyes only stayed upon the encroaching beings. "You two, take your mother and go!"

"I'm not leaving you!" Mary pleaded.

James slowly got to his feet. "I'm not going to have a debate, honey. Please, go with the boys!"

Mary began to sob hysterically. "I love you, James!"

"I love you too," he whispered. James began to reload the gun, the intruders nearly within reach.

As Idris and Cal began to escort their mother to safety, they heard rustling in the brush before them.

Idris stopped dead in his tracks. His heart began to race into a frenzy. "Both of you wait."

Everyone all waited.

Then the beings all came in the same fashion the others did.

With each of these...things, you could hear them humming to some unknown tune. All of them were all hunched over, sharing that same damn sadistic grin. On one, though, it was far too much, like it knew it was going to get one of the family members. The surprise is just which one was going to be the lucky winner of this hellish contest.

Idris shifted his gaze upon them, side by side, as they all took steps back away from the row of 'black coats.'

"We need to find another way," he whispered aloud.

Mary stepped before them; arms stretched to protect her children.

Idris and call both cried for their mother, "Mom, no!"

"I want both of you to run!"

Cal began to cry. Idris grabbed his brother's hand and started to bolt for the front of the diner.

Gunshots echoed in the back lot. Idris and Cal looked back to see their father rushing for Mary. Behind him, a hulking mass now pursued James. The ruby string was more abundant and fierce. No longer was it the ridiculous tap-dancing marionette—it was a beast beyond any recognition. The reddish-brown leathery skin shined in the moon's glow, the rain still falling. It must have stood at least twelve feet tall now—lanky arms, hunched over much like the 'black coats' were. Malformed claws protruded on its arms and legs, resembling spikes, or sickles. Still on its face was that fucking messed up grin. The eyes changed rapidly—yellow to red, to orange, and back to yellow. The thing was salivating as it pursued its prey.

James turned his head over his shoulder to see the thing in pursuit. He glanced back ahead to the "black coats" nearing his wife. He had a plan and doubted it would work, but the thought came to mind, I'll be damned if I'm going to sit by and do nothing!

"Mary," he shouted out.

A big smile stretched on Mary's face. "James, you're OK!"

He grabbed hold of his wife and pulled her back with him, allowing themselves to be surrounded.

Mary's stomach turned. "James? What are you doing?"

"I have an idea, but I can't promise anything," he panted.

The massive thing grew nearer to them as did the 'black coats.' If his idea worked now, it would be what saved them or doomed them. James noticed the gaze of the 'black coats' turn up towards the beast.

"Yes, it might just work!"

One by one, the beast grabbed a "black coat" and devoured them wholly. The break for James and Mary had at last come. They began their escape towards their children. James hobbled on. His stomach turned as he saw a thick red vine rush past him.

He shrieked his wife's name, "Mary!"

She had turned around, but it was already too late.

The thing had changed again, sprouting a new array of red vines—thicker and longer. Black ooze dripped onto the ground. It more closely resembled a giant blob that was forming fast.

The vine had a hold of Mary's left arm. The boys started to run towards their mother when she pleaded, "No, don't you dare! Both of you run! Get out of here. We love you both!"

Their father had begun unloading the remaining bullets into the thing. Mary sobbed hysterically—in pain…and at the lost salvation. However, it was all about to get worse for her.

Another vine rushed and grabbed her right leg. There was a tearing sound. Maybe it was her waitress' outfit. Maybe it was the sound of her muscles, bone, and tissue—her entire arm and leg were ripped right off. Ruby-red blood squirted and spurted across the dark grassy lawn. Mary's voice reached a hysterical feverish pitch as her scream fell silent.

"No, Mary!" James rushed to his wife's bloody side. He took his belt off, trying to use it as a tourniquet on her thigh…what remained of it. "Mary, no, oh God! Just hang on!"

She looked up at him. Her face now pale under the moonlight. Her body was shaking immensely, growing colder every passing moment. "I love you, James. I…am…so sorry."

He looked at her, perplexed. "Shh, shh, don't be." He kissed her forehead and caressed her head, rocking her in his arms. "Hang on, just hold on..."

She was dead.

The wandering cloud finally passed over, allowing the moon's light to shine once more.

James stared into the eyes of his wife. Hysteria began to set in, "No, no, no, no, no, NO, NO, NO!!"

A series of crimson vines clung to Mary's other left leg.

"You can't have her, you son of a bitch!"

James used the gun like a club and bashed the vines into a black-red bloody pulp, off of his wife's body. The thing seemed screech in pain, retracting the damaged appendages.

"I'll kill you!" He stumbled as he reached to his feet and removed the last four bullets from his pants pocket. Foaming and blinded with rage, he slowly walked towards the blob, aiming for that goddamn stupid grin. "Di—ie!"

The final four shots rang out.

At first, the thing seemed dead. It collapsed and did not stir. James started to laugh hysterically, unaware of what it was doing.

"Boys, boys, it's dead!" He yelled, laughing hysterically.

He was all alone.

He walked over to his wife's body. Blood soaked and in a pool of her own. He knelt beside her.

"Honey, I did it…I did it." He caressed her face, streaks of blood formed and followed his strokes.

James felt a strange sensation, and then nothing. He turned around to see the red vines digging into Mary's body, jerking it out of his arms.

James rushed to his feet, and in vain, attempted to go after her. "NO, NO, NO, GOD DAMN IT! NO!"

Into the very-much-alive thing, she went, causing him to drop to his knees.

It would soon change…again.

Much of the blob, or whatever the hell it was, fell to the ground. Inside the dark goo, was something else, something that tore at the darkness and demanded to be free. Finally, a hand punctured the makeshift bubble. It was human, or instead, at least it appeared to be. Inch by inch, more of the being became uncovered, and soon, James only gazed on in awe.

So beautiful. James searched for the words but only found silence.

It had become her.

Finally, she slowly rose up from the taint and approached James.

"Mary…"

Heat radiated off her (James' memory recalled the memories of the first time they showered together and the love they made) as she stood before him now, looking down. Her body, bare in the moonlight, with the rain steadily falling. Droplets ran down her cheeks, down her neck, conforming to the outlines of her breasts, arms, stomach, and legs. He touched her stomach, warm to the touch, and ran his fingers up and down her arms. Splotches of ebony and crimson still tainted her—the ashes from which she had risen from, reborn from the dark pitch of Hell—beautiful, radiant—a twisted phoenix. However, as much as James knew, she had died in his arms. He was aware that this was all wrong, that this wasn't his beloved.

He stood up before her, numb, whether it was the sensation of the vines that slowly were enveloping him, or if it was that everything was coming to an end, and it didn't matter anymore. He stared into her big blue eyes.

He ran his hands over her cheeks, "So cold…" They stared back, unwavering, perhaps searching and absorbing everything. He ran his fingers over her ruby lips. Memories continued to flood his mind, and with this, he was satisfied. James dropped his gaze. "If you're going to kill me…do it quick, please."

"I know you…" she muttered.

Surprise struck him, as he glanced back to her eyes, a sliver of hope presented itself. "You know me?"

"James…" she whispered.

"Mary, I am so sorry," he sobbed as he instinctively clung to her.

A sadistic grin sprawled across those ruby lips. "Yes…she tasted absolutely delicious, James."

His eyes widened as he pushed away from the doppelganger. Mary stared at him, noting the surprise, yet, confused. He knew that he was going to die, that had been from the start. He was with her, and that was all that mattered to him.

"You're not resisting? You're quite interesting." She continued to grin.

"It's all over. At least now, we can be together." James closed his eyes and embraced the false Mary once more. He felt the vines and twine that protruded from her back in a crude mockery of a pair of wings. They wrapped around him tightly, engulfing him wholly. As they constricted him, he could feel the popping and snapping of bones inside of him. He clung more forcibly to her.

He started to cough hard; blood began to pour from his nose and mouth. He retracted his breath; the vines had already wrapped around his torso and continuing their way up.

He stared into the cold eyes once more that squinted with that damn smile. "Before I go, I have something I want to give you."

There was a click, and then something fell to the ground. James smiled to himself. "Burn in Hell, you monster."

Mary, I'm sorry, and I love you.

The thing looked down at James' hand, but it was already too late. Much like it was for Mary before, this was the end, but for them both. James embraced her one last time. Its eyes widened as the explosion had been initiated and consumed them both wholly.

Under the dying rain, the moonlit twilight sky was bright and clear to emptiness. In a small radius from where the two stood, there was some disgusting confetti of what was James and the would-be Mary. Pieces, limbs, and all that were large enough to survive littered the diner's backyard. The ground was a thick porridge of sable, verdant and crimson pools. Nothing moved. Nothing sighed. Nothing.

It was finally all over.

***

Idris and Cal had gone inside the diner. They went into their father's office, taking the cash purse and two small handguns.

Idris handed Cal a gun while keeping one for himself. "Remember what I showed you, OK?"

Cal gave a nod, occasionally glancing over his shoulder. Fright was still on his face, as was a concern for his mother and father. Idris took note of this and had assumed the worst.

"Cal, I need you to be strong, OK? I know it's a lot to ask right now, but," Idris sighed, "we must do it for them. We need to survive."

Cal looked up at his big brother. "I know, it's just...it's hard."

"There will be a time to mourn after we see this through, OK? For now, we have to go and fast."

Idris grabbed a few boxes of ammunition and tossed it in a black knapsack. He also threw in a pair of hunting knives and miscellaneous snacks.

Idris crouched next to his little brother. "Now, we're going to sneak out front. I want you to run if anything gets too close to us, alright?"

Cal cocked his head. "Shouldn't we take the car?"

"That would allow them to know where we are. It's too risky," Idris ruffled Cal's hair, "but I give you props."

The two brothers wandered quietly to the front door and looked out the front parking lot. It had been quiet since he last heard his dad firing the gun and of...mom.

He scanned the front, checking past the entrance and the street. "Alright, it looks clear," Idris whispered.

"So, we should assume that something is waiting for us, right?" Cal gave his brother a serious expression.

Idris grinned. "Yeah, that's right, we should.

He glanced back outside and plotted a path. "OK, stay glued to me. We'll exit here, then along to the right side of the diner, and go straight towards the main road. Stick to the side of the road and then cross over to the shadows. Got it?"

Cal nodded. "Got it."

There was an explosion, which shook the diner. Pots and pans rattled, while various items on the shelves fell to the floor. Both brothers looked to one another, saddened, but yet hopeful.

"C'mon, let's go!" Idris whispered as he opened the front door.

Along the diner's front, they stuck to the shadows. They cut behind their grandfather's monument and headed for the main road. Everything seemed to be going well, too well, in fact.

They crossed the main road and started to run downtown. Looking back every so often, hoping for mom and dad, or watching as their parents drove to come and get them, and they would all get away safely. Idris shook his head clear of such fantasy. They were dead. He came to terms that this was their new life now. That this was how things were, and how it was going to be.

Cal tugged at his brother's sleeve, "Idris! Look!"

Idris turned around to see what it was Cal was so insisting on showing him. His eyes began to swell as he saw a lone figure walking towards them. It had stopped and then started to run.

Dad!

They both stood up and wandered into the street. However, part of Idris was uncertain, and he found it odd.

"Dad, we're over here," Cal shouted.

Idris' eyes widened. Fear had set in. He cupped his brother's mouth fast. "Shh, Cal, don't say another word. Turn around and run, now!"

Cal looked frightfully to his big brother, puzzled, but then saw the monstrosity that was encroaching fast.

"Boys, boys, I'm so glad you didn't stray too far!"

Cracks and snaps echoed from behind the running man, but Idris could see the same crimson vines and twine waving wildly under the moonlight, whipping against the ground violently. He pushed his brother, and both set off in full force for downtown.

James grinned fiercely, "Oh, how I do just love a little game of cat and mouse!"

Idris and Cal both ran frantically through the streets as it crept into the small downtown. On some alleyways, Idris noted that they were boarded up with some metal sheets.

What the hell is going on? Where is everyone?

They panted as they had stopped near a storm drain. Water rushed around them. Idris surveyed the area, believing to have lost their father.

We're near the water plant.

"Ah, ah, ah, come now, boys. Really? Did you honestly think you could outwit your old man?" James was behind them, the vines and twine lashed about wildly, hungry for the two survivors.

"You're not our father!" Cal yelled at the impostor.

He shrugged, smiling "Ah, you got me, kiddo," he threw his arms up, "but just so you know. Your daddy tried so hard to kill your mommy...well...me." He grinned that damn stupid grin. "Just look how that turned out—kudos for the suicide bombing effort, but really c'mon." it started to laugh and pace. "Oh, you humans, such pathetic, selfish, and wanna-be-righteous fanatics. You tarry on day after day, worrying about death, money, food, and the affairs and lifestyles of celebrities. You think that YOU are the only ones in this miserable little galaxy. You're all insignificant, nothing more than moths to a flame..." he stopped pacing, "well, in this case, my late-night snack, but besides that, you're just nothing but fodder."

Idris calmly spoke to the monster. "You will be stopped; the government will—"

"The government?" James began laughing hysterically. "I have a newsflash for you, kiddo. Haha, you think your government is protecting you? Spoilers—your precious government has made your town, your mommy, and daddy, and millions upon millions of humans, meals for me." His wicked smile shined brilliantly under the saddened moonlight.

The boys stared on in shock. "N—no, that can't be true! You're lying!"

"Ah, come now, boys. You should be grateful for some last moment father to sons bonding. Would your dear old dad lie to you?" He chuckled as he began pacing some more. "Think of it as feeding your small, delicious brains. After all, they say knowledge is power, and well, pumping up that little thing would just make it taste sweeter to me, mmm yes."

"What are you?" Idris asked disgustingly.

"Ah, ah, now that would be spoiling too much." he waved his index finger side to side. "Let's just say. I have an arrangement made. What you would call a deal with the devil. Oh, can you guess who I am in that part?"

Idris heard an engine trying to turn not too far away. Someone else is still in town! Idris's ears perked up, but so did the James'.

"Well, fancy that, I bet that's our uninvited guest. I've been looking for that one for some time now." James shook his head. "No matter, I can get him after I finish with you two."

Cal looked over at his big brother, who looked back at him. The crimson vines lashed against the ground violently, starting to sprawl across the land towards them.

"Well, it's been fun, boys, but it's now time for you to get in my belly!" James let loose a chuckle as he patted his stomach.

"Eat this!" Cal tossed Idris a grenade, one of the few they had taken from the old van. With finesse and precision, Idris lobbed it at their impostor of a father.

James bellowed condescendingly as the grenade landed at his feet, "You little sons of bitches!"

Although Idris and Cal had already turned tail and ran, the concussion of the blast sent them off their feet. They scrambled as they saw the black and red pools, and limbs reassembling together and heard it scream with a bloody vengeance.

"Alright, boys, playtime is officially over!"

They ran frantically through the outside of the water treatment plant. The cracking and hissing of something foreign, but on this night, well-known was in hot pursuit. It seemed to be coming everywhere around them.

"C'mon, Cal, we gotta find that truck!" Idris panted as they ran past more water pipes.

Suddenly, as they passed the last column of pipes, the ground beneath them burst open, along with the pipes. Idris and Cal landed separately from each other on the ground, the water surging, soaking them thoroughly.

"Here's daddy!" James cackled maniacally.

"Cal!" Idris looked up to see their father standing over his little brother. He scrambled to his feet and pulled his handgun out. "Argh!" he grunted as he fired a series of shots at the lashing monster of a man.

Cal scurried away on his back and then flipped himself over and began to run. He collapsed almost as fast as he had gotten to his feet. Cal looked down to find his ankle wrapped by one of the crimson vines. He felt an immense pressure build, and then it went numb.

"Idris," Cal cried.

James lunged for Idris, the bullets having hardly any effect on him. Idris rolled away and fired another series of shots, two piercing the impostor's head, dropping it to the ground.

"Hang on, Cal!" Idris ran over to his brother, stomping the vine into the asphalt.

"My foot, I can't feel it." Cal looked up at his brother, feeling like he let his brother down.

"It's OK, Cal, but we have to go. Hang on tight, alright?" Idris knelt and picked his brother up via piggy-back.

The truck had begun to move, and it was nearby. Idris carried Cal and hurried towards the back exit.

Meanwhile, slowly the vines began to lash in their frenzied assault. "I grow so, so very tired of you two insects. And look, now I am all wet!" James shook his hands. "You are—ugh— you're so going to be grounded—indefinitely!"

They had rounded the corner, and just in time. The truck was approaching the brothers fast but had to slow for the turn out of the exit.

"Get ready!" Idris readjusted carrying his brother. "Grab on, and then I'll get on, alright?"

His little brother clenched him tightly, "OK!"

Idris started to run towards a nearby truck. It wasn't the regular water tank carrier or the usual delivery truck; it was one of the freighter carriers who delivered to the neighboring towns. He'd seen it go by now and then back at the diner, or when Old Joe used to stop in sometimes. It had an extended trailer, with the two front panels that would slide up and down. Thankfully, they were already up.

The truck slowed down as it approached the gate, the headlights bright—gazing upon them. Then something they didn't expect happened.

A man yelled out to them, "Get in, quick!"

Idris ran to the passenger-side door and hoisted Cal up, before getting in himself. He closed the door, and the truck resumed its onslaught on the gate, bashing it wide open. Behind them, a dark, twisted evil silhouette fell upon the asphalt that led from the back-parking lot to the exit. He still had that damn sadistic grin.

"I was wondering when you two would show up." The driver glanced over at the two brothers.

He was unclean, very rugged. He had somewhat long dark hair and a full bushy beard. He smelled like he hadn't taken a shower in days if not weeks, and reeked of whiskey. He wore a red-black checkered flannel with a black baseball cap. "You can call me Mac."

"What the hell is going on, Mac? Who or what was that—that thing?" Idris looked over at their newfound friend and savior.

"Ha, wish I could tell ya, kid. I can't exactly say what it is or where it came from...but it's from space, and it gets hungry, and it changes faces more than an infant in diapers. Some folks do know, but they're a...little hard to reach." Mac reached down and grabbed his bottle of whiskey and took a swig. "Sorry to have brought you, kids, into this mess."

Idris and Cal both looked over at Mac. "What do you mean?" Idris inquired.

Mac sighed heavily. "That van was mine, all my research and well, my arsenal and then some. Everything in that shit of a heap was mine."

Idris restrained himself. "So, you mean to say that you're the reason our parents are dead, and why the town is pretty much dead?"

Mac shook his head. "Yes, and no. Yes, because I was tracked there, but no, since they were going to visit it regardless of my presence. You see. It gets a free lunch card pass, and well. It happened to be your town's day. Think of it as an ambassador with diplomatic immunity, in this case, intergalactic immunity, who can say whatever it wants. I had hoped the timer, and my card would have given enough incentive to book it."

"But there was a woman my dad talked to, Cheryl Plain. The police said it was her van." Idris looked ahead on the road.

Mac grunted as he cleared his throat. "Cheryl? Ha, that S.O.S. was the kill order if anything. If you want to be angry with anyone, be so with the "police" and whoever your daddy talked to. Don't get me wrong; she was the broad that authorized that thing to clean out hundreds of towns, but she was taken care of months ago. I can vouch for that. Whoever gave the go-ahead this time around, well, I ain't got the slightest clue."

Idris clenched his hands. Cal looked at his brother. "Idris, I'm tired."

"Do yourselves a favor, get some sleep. You're going to need it." Mac shifted the truck's gears; the small town of

Lodestone was now a speck behind them. The moon was high, with the road desolate and the land, a dull green, open and wide, for miles all around them. Ahead of them were the peaks of mountains, reaching up for the umbrella of stars. The storm had passed, and again, Idris found the prelude he felt earlier was right. This predicament had evolved into a shitstorm far more than anyone could ever imagine, and it had only just begun.

"Thanks, Mac." Idris readjusted himself, still holding the gun, concealing it.

Mac grinned. "Don't mention it. We'll sort out the details in the morning. For now, though, put that thing away, you're making me nervous."

"Sorry, I just don't know who to trust," Idris replied.

"I know that all too well, kid. Trust me." Mac sighed.

The truck sped on the desolate backwater road through the night.

Chapter Four

OUTSIDE OF LODESTONE, on its eastern border, there sat a white van. The road into town had been barricaded, as were the other main entries.

Inside the van, there was a team of five men. They all stared at the images of the bloodied town. Well, all but one man. This one sat thinking, with his head heavy on one hand. While the others around spoke of success and congratulated each other on a job 'well done,' this one watched the monitor of a semi-truck going west along some backwater road.

Idiots, they don't even know yet. Ugh, this whole operation, let alone the idea of working with those...those things—make me sick!

He removed his glasses and rubbed his tired eyes. Another man turned around and patted him on the back.

"Cheer up, Ian! Don't be such a Debbie Downer."

Ian glared at the man. "Frank, I suggest if you value the use of your hand, instead of your wife, you will leave me alone."

Frank's brow had formed to anger before the others convinced him to 'leave him alone.'

A phone rang nearby the field teams' supervisor. "Shh, shh, it's him." The van's commotion quieted down as he initiated the conversation. "Sir?"

"How did the operation fair?"

The supervisor gave a thumbs-up to his team. "It went very well, sir. Precisely, to plan."

"And what of the van?"

"It's in our possession, the research, documentation, everything, sir."

"Good…" there was a fatally calm pause, "Were there any survivors?"

"No, sir, all were assimilated by TS-21. The replacements will arrive at 0700, and cleanup is already underway."

Then, there was an awkward silence that befell inside the van.

"Mr. Murdoch, congratulations, you've just been promoted."

The men all looked back at Ian, who had already readied his gun.

"I told you miserable gnats that I wanted no survivors, and you go and let two little brats escape!" the man's voice on the end of the line grew furious. "Your services are no longer required, gentlemen. Be thankful I don't dispose of you to TS-21 or any other of those celestial walking trash bins!"

Frank and the others all pleaded with Ian. "Sorry, boys, orders are orders, and I finally get my very own parking spot."

Ian fired four shots into the heads of his former comrades.

"Follow them, and see if there's anything useful that can be acquired. I want you to report to me in two hours," the voice commanded.

"I understand, sir. I do know this. He...is with the boys, and they have the disk." Ian cleaned off his gun and wiped the sparse specks of blood off his face with a handkerchief.

The voice seemed to growl in reply. "Keep an eye on them and move when necessary; I don't want any more screw-ups. If this gets out, then we will have a serious bullshit factor that I seriously do not need. Do whatever you deem necessary to get the job done." The man sighed over the line. "Why is good help such a hard thing to find these days?"

"Excuse me, sir, but what about TS-21?" Ian pushed a button that projected a very bored 'James.' He looked up at the sky, grinning, seemingly knowing he was being watched.

The man on the phone grunted. "Eradicate it. There are too many of these, elitist vermin running amok. Thinking that due to this arrangement, they can do whatever the hell they want. Just get rid of it."

Ian nodded to the invisible man, "Understood, sir."

As Ian motioned to disconnect the line, the man spoke once more. "Oh, and Mr. Murdoch?"

"Sir?"

"Don't fuck this up, or I will end you." the man's voice then changed to a cheery tone, "Congratulations again on your promotion."

There was a click, followed by silence. Ian looked at the monitor of James and pressed a button on the control panel off to the right. James frantically patted himself, then angrily yelled up towards the satellite camera, before erupting into a massive pool of chromatic blood onto the ground.

Ian sighed, flipping the monitor off. He looked over at the dead bodies of Frank and the others. "I guess I should have told you, Frank. Your wife was pretty damn good last night, but hey, maybe you shouldn't have been sleeping around."

Ian exited out the back doors of the van and walked over towards a black car that parked a small distance from the van. He got in the car and closed the door. Pulling a black sleeve up, and revealing a silver wristwatch—his pale complexion in a glimpse of the time. He dug for a small remote in his coat pocket, and pressed a series of buttons, detonating the van into oblivion.

He put on his black leather gloves before adjusting the rear-view mirror. A glimpse of his bright green eyes and short dark brown hair, clean and well kept. He turned the ignition, and with haste, tore off in pursuit of the Lodestone Municipal Water truck.

Ian sighed as he drove the car hard. *Why do I feel that this whole thing is not going to end well for anyone?*

He shook his head, vainly attempting to erase any doubt about his job and of morals. After all, he just got promoted and was on the track of going up the chain. Still, he couldn't help but shake the feeling that TS-21 wasn't dead, no matter what the higher-ups said about the process of elimination. The fact, though, that he, let alone they, were allowing these acts to carry on.

He switched the radio on, strumming his fingers to an old rock song that sang about a "…wayward son." It would be dawn in a few hours, and he had two brothers, along with a wanted man on his to-do list.

Elsewhere, *something* was reforming, and it had a slew of people on its to-do list, and it had all the time in the world to spare.

Acknowledgments

Thanks to my wife for putting up with my shenanigans. You're amazing.

I would like to thank the members of Morphine and friends. Thank you for all the wonderful music you guys have produced and to Mark Sandman [Rest in Peace].

Thanks to Buckethead for fueling me with countless hours of great music on this project and others.

Thanks to my friends for your continued support.

John Carpenter for his adaptation of *Who Goes There?* as the 1982 classic *The Thing*.

John W. Campbell for penning *Who Goes There?* and paving the way for a fantastic franchise.

Those involved with *The Thing from Another World* and *The Thing [2011]*.

My *World of Warcraft* friends on the US server Aegwynn, and in the Horde guild, Revolt. You're all demoted to 'Village Bicycle.'

With love,

Sin

Anyone else I may have forgotten to mention...thank you.

About the Author

Robert J. S. T. McCartney loves to write about the strange and bizarre. The urban fantasy novel *Lilah's Guide to Hoyle* was written in collaboration with his friend and co-author, Albert Debusschere III. He currently lives in Knoxville, Tennessee with his wife and kids.

He is the author of the *Among Us: Contact, Assimilation, Control, Extermination Series*, *The Chronicles of Bob: The Chronic Suicidal*, *Abnormal Side Effects*, and other stories.

He also plays *World of Warcraft* and loves some sweet tunes.

A.B.Normal
Publishing and Media Group
Anything but normal.

Visit us at www.abnormalpublishing.com for more stories.

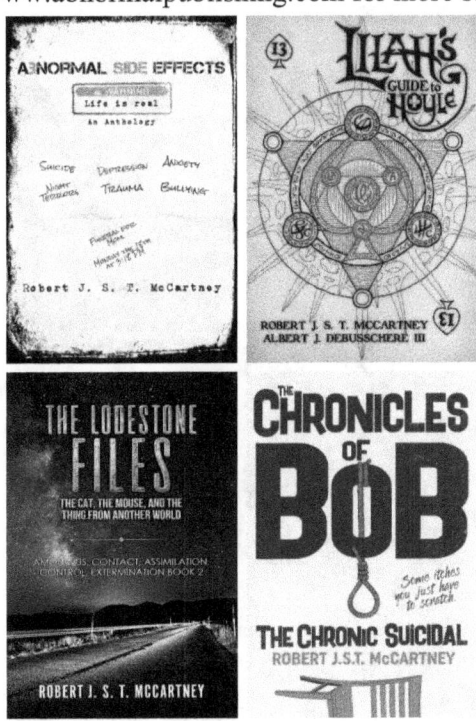

www.ingramcontent.com/pod-product-compliance
Lightning Source LLC
Chambersburg PA
CBHW052144220626
47052CB00005B/1188